THE WAY HOME

Karen Leah Scott

This book is a work of fiction. Names, characters, places, and incidents either are products of the author's imagination or are used fictitiously. Any resemblance to actual persons, living or dead, events, or locales is entirely coincidental.

Chapter 1

Mary sat beside the lifeless body of her father, clinging to his hand, her heart heavy with a mixture of sorrow and relief. Finally, he was out of pain and gone to be with God. She reached out and stroked the few wisps of grey hair off his forehead, sniffling as she did.

"Be with God, Papa," she whispered softly, her voice quivering. "Say hi to Ma for me."

The soft creak of the door opening caught her attention, and she looked up to see the nurse poking her head into the room. Her kind face was etched with concern.

"Is he gone?" the nurse asked gently, her voice barely above a whisper as if not to disturb the profound silence that had settled over the room.

Standing, Mary responded, "Yes, please call the doctor so that he can make the necessary arrangements."

As the nurse left the room, Mary leaned back in her chair and closed her tired eyes. The last few weeks, she had been particularly grueling, filled with sleepless nights and constant worry as she awaited the inevitable. Now that it was over, a wave of exhaustion washed over her. She was thankful that her father's suffering had ended, but an overwhelming sense of loss and fear crept in. She was alone now, truly alone. With no other relatives or siblings, she had spent the last two years devotedly caring for her father, watching him gradually wither away.

The sound of approaching footsteps gently pulled her back to the present. Doc Murphy entered the room, his eyes full of professional empathy.

"I'm so sorry for your loss," he said softly as he neared her. "Is there anyone you want me to call?"

Mary shook her head slowly. "No, Doctor. It's just me. What do I do now?"

Doc Murphy's face remained kind as he gently pulled the sheet over her father's face. "I'll reach out to the undertaker for you. He'll come and take care of everything. I assume your father made all the necessary arrangements?"

"Yes, he did. Everything is arranged," Mary replied, her hands clutching her purse as if it were her lifeline to reality in that moment. "I think I'll go home now and get some rest."

"That sounds like a good idea, Mary," Doc Murphy said gently. "I'll talk to Undertaker, and you'll probably need to contact Ed Whitaker for the will," he added, offering a small guiding hand in her confusion.

Mary nodded again, feeling numb. The reality of her solitude was beginning to sink in, and she knew the days ahead would be challenging. As she stood up and prepared to leave, she took one last look at her father's covered form, whispering a final goodbye.

The walk to her buggy was surreal. The hospital corridors were a blur of white walls and muted lighting, stark contrasts to the turmoil in her heart. Each step felt heavy, laden with the weight of loss and the unknown future that stretched out before her.

Outside, the world continued to spin. People walked by, engaged in their own lives, unaware of the profound change that had just occurred in hers. As she drove home, the familiar streets felt strangely foreign. The home she had shared with her father for so long now felt like an empty shell.

She opened the door and stepped inside, the house's silence pressing down on her. Everywhere she looked, there were reminders of him – the chair he used to sit in, the blanket he loved, the books he never got to finish. She walked slowly through each room, her mind flooded with memories – some sweet, some painful.

She had been his sole caregiver after he fell ill, steadfastly refusing to let anyone else lift a finger. The days raced by in a blur as she balanced nursing him with the demands of her job at the factory, a constant struggle that wore her down, bit by bit. Exhaustion enveloped her, both physically and emotionally. Walking into the living room, she sank onto the couch, closing her eyes and letting out a deep sigh. She knew she needed to rest, but sleep was elusive. The quiet of the house was now a constant reminder of her new reality.

Although Mary had never discussed the arrangements her father had made, she assumed, as his only child, that he had left everything to her—his fortune and the house. They were not wealthy by any means, but they had been comfortable. Mary felt confident that her father had ensured she would be provided for after his death.

She knew she had to be strong and face the tasks ahead – calling Ed Whitaker, dealing with the funeral arrangements, and figuring out how to move forward alone. But for now, all she could do was sit and allow herself to grieve, to feel the depth of her loss.

Tomorrow would bring a new day with new challenges, but for tonight, she allowed herself to mourn the end of an era, the loss of the man who had been her anchor and her guide through life. And though she felt alone, she whispered a quiet prayer, hoping that her parents were watching over her somewhere, giving her the strength to carry on.

MARY SAT STARING IN disbelief across the desk at Ed Whitaker. "I don't understand."

"I'm sorry, Mary," Ed Whitaker, the lawyer, shifted the papers in his hand and looked at her. "Your father had some serious gambling debts and has indicated that the house and property be sold to pay them off upon his death."

Mary frowned. "But you mean he hasn't made any provisions for me?"

Shaking his head, Ed said, "Sorry. The house and property are to go up for sale, and the money will be sent to the bank to cover his debt. There is no mention of anything going to you other than a few personal items, but he did leave you this," Ed added, holding out a brown envelope with her name written on it.

Sighing, Mary took it and thanked the lawyer. Her head ached, and she needed to think. How could her father have done that to her? She had been so good to him in his last few months, and he was always telling her what a good daughter she was, all the time knowing that he hadn't left her anything.

When she got home, she unhooked the buggy from the horse and put him in his stall for the night. Wearily walking into the house, she closed and locked the door, leaning her head against the door frame. She was exhausted and in desperate need of a cup of tea.

Her father had always been a sensible man, working hard to support his family. As a young man, he worked endlessly, doing whatever job he could find until he saved up enough money to buy a house with a small parcel of land.

As a young child, Mary grew up thinking they were rich beyond means. They were one of the many houses in town that had running water. Her father always took great pride in the fact he provided well for his family.

After her mother got sick and died, her father seemed to change. He no longer had the drive or passion for working his land and would leave in the evening, disappearing for hours, making Mary wonder where he spent his time. She now knew where he had gone each night.

Driven by an unwavering resolve to support her family, she took the initiative and secured a job at the local factory. The new position was demanding and often required long hours, but Mary embraced it wholeheartedly. Though her paycheck wasn't huge, it represented much more than just a sum of money; it was a lifeline. Each dollar earned went towards ensuring that the lights stayed on, food remained on the table, and the bills were paid on time. In a world where every cent counted, Mary's contribution brought a sense of stability and hope to her household.

Lighting the wood stove, she filled the kettle with water, the sound of cold metal clinking against the tap echoing in the quaint kitchen.

The kettle, a worn heirloom, rich with memories of countless cups of tea shared and stories told, found its place on the stove. Walking over, she envisioned her mother making her tea countless times in the past before sinking into the old wooden chair by the window. The letter lay before her, its plain envelope a stark contrast to the turmoil within her heart.

As she ripped open the envelope, the paper resisting slightly against her anxious fingers, she couldn't help but wonder what her father could have to say to her from beyond the grave. The familiar script on the letter, so like him, was a stab of nostalgia. She took a deep breath, steeling herself for the words she might not be ready to read.

Dear Mary,

I'm so sorry for what I have done. It wasn't supposed to be this way, but I had to do what I had to do. It was either to pay off the debt or leave you with the burden. I know you are a strong girl and will figure out a way to carry on in life. Please remember that I love you.

Your Pa.

Tears welled up, unbidden, blurring the ink slightly as she read and re-read the words. Her father's apology, tinged with regret, hit her like a physical blow. She felt a surge of anger, confusion, and an overwhelming grief all at once. The kettle began to whistle, a sharp, almost accusatory sound that jolted her back to reality.

She rose, mechanically moving to take the kettle off the stove, pouring the boiling water into a chipped teapot. Her movements steady, though her mind was far from calm. As she let the tea steep, she pondered her father's actions and the heavy legacy of debt now resting on her shoulders. Each sentence of the letter replayed in her mind, her father's love and sorrow intertwined in those final written words.

The house was silent, save for the ticking of the old clock on the mantle and the occasional crackle from the stove. As she poured herself a cup of tea, she felt the weight of responsibility settling heavily upon her. Yet, beneath the sadness, a flicker of determination sparked. She had her father's strength running through her veins, and despite the hardships, she would find a way to move forward. Mary knew that life would not be easy, but she vowed to honor her father's sacrifice by forging ahead, one step at a time.

With a deep breath, she set the letter down on the worn table, its weight a little lighter now. She sipped her tea, the warmth spreading through her, fortifying her spirit. Outside, the first rays of dawn began to pierce through the grey, promising a new day and, with it, a glimmer of hope.

Mary sat staring at her father's scrawled handwriting, feeling empty inside. Strong? Her father called her strong. She was no stronger than he was. What was she going to do now? Here she was, twenty-two, single, alone with no chance for any happiness, and now the only place she called home was being ripped from under her.

Tears welled in her eyes, blurring the words on the page. The memories of the nights she spent by her father's bedside, the quiet conversations, the stories from his younger days, all seemed hollow now. She had believed in him, taken solace in his reassurances, but it had all been a lie. Or perhaps, as she tried to convince herself, he had been too ashamed to admit the truth.

The kettle whistled sharply, breaking her daydream. Mary wiped her eyes and got up to make her tea. She needed the warmth, the comfort it would bring, and maybe, just maybe, some clarity.

She stared out the kitchen window, watching the sun dip below the horizon, casting long shadows over the field that would no longer be hers. The grief she felt wasn't just for the property, but for the life she thought she would have, the future she had envisioned. She felt the weight of her father's choices, and the burden he had handed down to her.

As the tea steeped, Mary considered her options. She could fight the sale, but with what resources? And to what end? Her father's debts were not imaginary; they were real and loomed large over her future. Or, she could leave and start anew somewhere far from here, where the memories of her father's betrayal wouldn't haunt her.

But even as these thoughts crossed her mind, Mary felt a surge of defiance rising within her. Perhaps her father was right about one thing: she was strong. She cared for him, managed the household, and supported herself without complaint. She could do this. She could find a way.

The envelope lay open on the table, the letter still in her hand. An idea began to form. What if she could buy the property herself? It was a long shot, but maybe there was someone who could help her with a loan. She wasn't without skills or determination, and the land, though it needed work, had potential. Maybe she could make her father's dream of growing crops a reality, not just for him, but for herself.

The weight of despair began to lift, replaced by a spark of hope. She sipped her tea slowly, feeling the warmth spread through her. The road ahead would be challenging, but Mary Whitaker was no stranger to hard work. She had a plan to make.

AS MARY STEPPED OUT into the sunshine, she found herself grateful for the distraction that her visit to the store had provided—however brief. The warmth on her face was a stark contrast to the chill she felt inside whenever she thought about her uncertain future. With the Matrimonial Newspaper tucked securely under her arm, she started making her way back home, the wheels in her mind turning over the possibilities that now seemed at hand.

Her father's passing had left her with an unexpected and overwhelming responsibility. Though valuable, the house and the land were constant reminders of dreams unfulfilled and opportunities squandered. Mary sighed as she walked, each step crunching on the gravel road serving as a rhythmic counterpoint to her racing thoughts.

Was she really ready to sell everything and leave the only home she'd ever known? Where would she go? This was the only home she knew.

After securing her horse and buggy in the barn, Mary paused to take in the fields that stretched before her. Despite her father never having farmed the land, she could see the potential it held. Lush green grasses swayed gently with the breeze, a testament to the fertility of the soil. In different circumstances, she might have reveled in the challenges and rewards of tending to such a bountiful earth. But the reality was stark—without the means or the hands to till the land, she knew she had little choice but to let it go.

Entering the house, with its familiar creak of the floorboards, Mary felt a pang of nostalgia mixed with trepidation. She placed her parcels on the kitchen table, her gaze lingering on the paper once more. Mail-order brides. The concept seemed so foreign yet oddly enticing. Was this truly the solution to her troubles? The promise of starting over, even if in an unconventional way, held a flicker of hope that she couldn't easily dismiss.

Setting aside the practicality of the matter, Mary allowed herself a moment of fantasy. She imagined arriving in a new town and meeting a kind-hearted stranger who would be more than a rescuer—a partner, a confidant, perhaps even a soul mate. Could she be so lucky, or was she grasping at straws?

Her musings were interrupted by the sudden clatter of horse hooves approaching. Peering out the window, she saw the familiar figure of Mr. Whitaker, the town's lawyer and executor of her father's will. His stern expression softened somewhat when he saw her, but Mary knew this visit was likely to bring more news about her impending sale.

"Good afternoon, Mr. Whitaker," she greeted him at the door.

"Good afternoon, Mary," he replied, tipping his hat. "May I come in?"

"Of course," she answered, stepping aside to let him enter. As they settled into the parlor, Mary couldn't help but feel a sense of dread.

"I've reviewed the terms of your father's estate," Mr. Whitaker began, his tone professional but not unkind. "Given the circumstances, we must move forward quickly with the sale. Your financial obligations won't allow for much delay."

Mary nodded. "I understand. It's just...this place holds so many memories."

"I realize it's not easy," Mr. Whitaker sympathized. "But sometimes, a fresh start can be the best way to honor those memories while creating new ones."

As he spoke, Mary's thoughts drifted back to the Matrimonial Newspaper. Perhaps a fresh start was indeed what she needed—one bold step towards a future free from the shadows of her past.

"I suggest you start packing your belongings and anything else you want to bring with you."

"Thank you, Mr. Whitaker," she said, her resolve hardening. "I'll be ready for the sale."

After he left, Mary sat quietly for a moment, feeling a mixture of anxiety and determination. Finally, she reached for the newspaper, opened to the center page, and began to read the personal ads for Mail Order Brides in earnest. Perhaps, just perhaps, there was a glimmer of hope amidst the uncertainty, a chance to build a new life on her own terms.

It was with that glimmer that Mary let herself dream again, dreaming of a future where she could once more find joy, purpose, and perhaps, against all odds—love.

Chapter 2

Mary stood at the threshold of her past, her fingers lingering on the doorknob of the only home she had ever known. The wood felt smooth under her touch, worn down by years of familiar handling. Each nick and scratch in the paint was a testament to the life lived within these walls—every birthday, every holiday, every tear and every laugh. She took a deep breath, the air thick with the scent of memories—freshly baked bread, her father's old cologne, the lavender her mother favored.

Putting the last piece of clothing into her suitcase, she stood up. "I don't think I can fit anything else in here," Mary said, her voice tinged with resignation as she turned back to her friend Susan. Boxes and trunks surrounded the two women, the physical remnants of a life left behind. "Everything else can be sold with the house."

Susan's eyes were wide with concern as she reached out, her hand resting on Mary's arm. "Oh, Mary. I really wish you would reconsider all of this. A Mail Order Bride. You don't know what you are getting into, going to live with a complete stranger and in the middle of nowhere."

Mary met Susan's gaze, seeing the worry etched in her friend's features. "I know, but what else do I have here? I'll never marry unless I'm willing to settle for Percy. The factory where I work is closing, so I don't even have a job anymore, and in a few days, I probably won't have any place to live."

"You can live with us, you know. I already talked it over with Jake, and he said it was okay," Susan said, her voice a mix of hope and desperation as she plopped down on the bed, causing the mattress to dip under her weight.

Mary shook her head, a sad smile playing on her lips. "You have enough on your plate with three kids and twins on the way. Besides, your Ma is moving this way to help you, so it would be too crowded."

"A complete stranger. Mary. What if? What if he is mean," Susan stammered.

"He sounds wonderful," Mary replied, smiled. "A very caring and compassionate man. I feel good about this."

Their conversation was interrupted by Jake's voice from the bedroom door. "Is your suitcase all ready to go, Mary? We should be going if you want to catch your train."

Mary leaped to her feet, her heart pounding with a mix of excitement and fear. She closed the trunk containing her clothes and memories, her fingers trembling slightly. "All set, Jake. Thanks."

Looking at Jake, she pointed to the boxes. "Those can go in storage until I write for them. All I'm bringing is this trunk and my suitcase."

Jake nodded picked up the trunk and nodded to her. "I'll let you say your goodbyes, and I'll meet you at the wagon."

Turning back to Susan, Mary forced a brave smile. "I guess this is it. I promise I'll write when I get there."

Tears welled up in Susan's eyes as she tried to smile back. "You better because you know how I will worry. I just hope you are safe."

Mary hugged her friend tightly, feeling the warmth and comfort of the familiar embrace. "I promise I'll let you know everything."

With heavy hearts, the two women walked downstairs together. Mary paused in the hallway, her eyes sweeping over the familiar surroundings one last time. The walls, once filled with laughter and life, now seemed hollow and silent. Her throat tightened as she opened the front door, stepping out into the crisp, uncertain air of her future.

Her life here had ended, and she was on to make new memories somewhere else. The path ahead was unknown, but in her heart, Mary held onto hope. She climbed into the carriage waiting outside, the wheels creaking under the weight of her belongings and the heavy burden of her past.

As the carriage pulled away, Mary looked back one last time, watching her home fade into the distance. With a deep breath, she faced forward, ready to embrace whatever lay ahead. The journey would be long, the destination uncertain, but Mary knew she had the strength to face whatever challenges came her way. Someday, she hoped, she would look back on this moment not with sadness but with gratitude for the new life and new memories she would create.

"COME HERE AND LET ME take a look at you," Casey called out to Preston. "You have to look half decent; you know."

Preston Wilson walked out of the bedroom and looked at his lifelong friend, Casey. He had known her for almost thirty years, and although she had married his best friend, their friendship was unbreakable.

"She sounds right pretty from her letters. What if she doesn't want an old cowboy like me," Preston said as he adjusted his cowboy hat on his head.

Casey looked Preston up and down and frowned. "Good lord Preston, you aren't old and hey, are those the same pants you wore cleaning out the barn yesterday?"

Preston looked down at his pants. "They're still clean. I dusted them off."

Putting her hands on her hips, Casey glared at him. "You want this girl to like you, not turn and run. Go change into a clean pair of pants, and while you're there, comb your hair. If you won't let me cut it, at least comb it. You don't want her thinking you're a savage."

MARY LOOKED OUT THE window at the crowd of people standing on the train platform. Although Preston had described himself, and she had an idea of what he looked like, none of the men standing on the platform fit the description. She imagined him being tall, with a head of curly dark hair, sharp facial features, and a look about him that would make a bear turn and run in fright. She imagined him strong and masculine, the type of man any woman would want.

Stepping off the train, she stood, looking around, her heart pounding in her chest as the reality of what she was doing finally hit her.

"Excuse me, are you Mary Johnson?" a female voice said from behind her as she stood on the platform.

Turning, Mary smiled. "Yes, I am, and you are?"

"Casey. Casey Brendon," Casey said, holding out her hand. "It's a real pleasure to meet you finally."

"I'm supposed to meet a Preston Wilson," Mary said, looking a bit confused.

"Yes, I'm a friend of Preston's, and you'll be staying with me till the Preacher can marry you," Casey said, picking up Mary's suitcase. "Is this all you have?"

"No, I have a trunk just being unloaded," Mary answered, still slightly confused. "Right over here."

"Perfect, we'll drive by and pick it up on our way home," Casey smiled. "Preston couldn't find a place to hitch the wagon, so he's waiting."

Walking towards the buggy, Mary could see a man sitting looking her way. As he saw them, he jumped down and took off his hat, watching the two women walk towards him.

"Preston, this is Mary," Casey said, putting Mary's suitcase in the back of the buggy.

Mary smiled at Preston and held out her hand. "Pleased to meet you, Mr. Wilson."

"Awwww, you can call me Preston. You sure are pretty," Preston said, taking Mary's hand and giving it a vigorous shake, making Casey stifle a laugh.

Mary continued to smile, not knowing what else to say. Preston was not really what she expected. He was tall, that was for sure, and from the first look, he was very muscular, but his hair was wild and unkempt, and most of his face was hidden behind months of beard growth. His clothes, although clean, were wrinkled and well-worn, and his boots had seen better days.

Helping her into the wagon, he turned and looked at her. "I've made arrangements with Casey for you to spend the night at her place. The Preacher will be able to marry us tomorrow when he gets back," he said, flicking the reigns.

Mary could feel her heart beat a mile a minute, wondering if she had made the right choice. Casey looked friendly enough, but Preston was not at all what she imagined.

"Don't worry, Mary. I'll take good care of you tonight. It'll be good to bond with you," Casey said from the back of the wagon where she was sitting. "We'll get to know each other real good."

Mary smiled at Casey and then turned to look at Preston. "You mentioned taking care of someone in your letters?" Mary asked.

Preston's stone face broke out in a smile. "Aww yes. Sweet Annie. She's my sister's baby. She lives with me now since Ma passed. It's just Annie and me, so that's who you'll be caring for. She's the sweetest little thing ever. When she looks at you, she melts your heart," Preston said. "You'll meet her tomorrow when I bring you home."

"How old is Annie?" Mary asked.

"Going on six months now and really smart," Preston beamed.

Mary thought to herself. *A baby? I don't have much experience with babies, and the thought of taking care of someone else's baby didn't really appeal to her. I wish I had known, I might not have written him back.*

Pulling up in front of Casey's home, Preston quickly unloaded the trunk and said his goodbyes, leaving the two women alone at the door.

Casey shook her head. "It'll do him good having a woman around. It will teach him some manners," Casey said, opening the door. "Come on in and get yourself settled. I'll make us some tea."

Mary walked into the house and looked around. It wasn't a big house, but it was homey and had a cozy feel to it. It consisted of a large room with a living area and a cooking area and off to the side, Mary could see a bedroom.

"You live here by yourself?" Mary asked, taking off her gloves.

"No. I have a husband, but he's away right now. He helps run cattle drives for some of the ranchers up the way. He won't be home until tomorrow," Casey said, indicating the chair for Mary to sit on. "We haven't been blessed yet with any youngins so, for now, it's just the two of us. You can put your suitcase in there," Casey pointed to the bedroom.

"I don't want to put you out," Mary shook her head.

"No bother. I'll sleep out here. It won't be my first time sleeping on that floor."

Coming back out of the bedroom, Mary sat down at the small table. "How do you know Preston?"

"It's going on almost thirty years, I reckon. I met him in school, and we've been like kin ever since," Casey said, putting two cups and saucers on the table. "Preston is a good man, Mary. He may be a bit awkward at times, but he's a good man, and you'll be taken care of."

Mary smiled. "He's not what I imagined. He sounded more.... Not sure what word I'm looking for."

"Sophisticated," Casey smiled. "I helped him write those letters. Heaven forbid you'd have never come if he had written them."

Mary laughed as she added milk to her tea. "I still can't believe I'm here."

"Well, I must say it'll be nice to have someone to talk with. I spend a lot of time with men, mostly because there aren't a lot of women around here. I used to get on with Preston's sister until she died," Casey said, sitting down.

"How did she die?" Mary asked.

"She and her husband were killed in a hold-up. Both shot dead. It was a terrible tragedy," Casey said, pouring hot water into two cups. "Becky and Joe loved Annie and they were such a cute couple."

"And Preston's mother?"

Casey shrugged. "Old age I guess. Preston found her sitting in her chair one day. It's like her body just gave up. It was hard on Preston and still is."

As Mary lay in bed that night, the weight of the day's revelations pressed heavily on her chest, making it hard to breathe easily. The gentle murmur of the night—crickets chirping, the soft rustling of leaves—was a stark contrast to the storm of thoughts swirling in her mind.

She couldn't help but think back to Casey's words. Becky and Joe's tragic end was haunting, but it was the courage and resilience of those left behind that truly struck her. Preston, a man she'd yet to know, had faced so much loss and yet still found the strength to care for Annie and keep the farm running. It was clear that he was a man of deep responsibility and commitment.

"Can I really make a life here?" Mary whispered into the darkness, her voice barely audible even to herself. Her mind drifted to her own father's farm, the place she'd called home all her life. It had been a modest plot compared to the expansive fields described by Casey, but it had been hers. She remembered the worn wooden fence posts, the lowing of cattle in the distance, and the rich smell of fertile soil after rain. And she remembered her father, a man of few words, who worked tirelessly until his unexpected addiction, one that drained their finances and left her with decisions she never thought she'd have to make.

The memories tugged at her heart, but they also reminded her why she had responded to the ad in the first place. There was nothing left for her back home, nothing but unpaid debts and whispered gossip. Here, she had a chance to start anew, to build something meaningful, even if it wasn't exactly what she'd dreamed of.

Talking to Casey had felt like speaking to an old friend, not someone she'd just met. There was a warmth in Casey's eyes that spoke of understanding and a life full of its own hardships and joys. "You'll see. Once you get to know him, you'll love him," she had said with so much conviction that Mary almost believed it then and there. But love was such a fragile, elusive thing. Could it really be found in such an arranged circumstance?

Mary's thoughts then wandered to Annie, the innocent soul who had already lost so much in her young life. Could she be a mother to this child? The idea was daunting, but the notion of bringing comfort and stability to Annie's life sparked a sense of purpose within her.

Her pulse quickened as she resolved to make the best of the situation. If not for herself, then for Annie and perhaps, in time, for Preston too. She pictured Annie's little hands holding hers, and the image brought an unexpected smile to her lips. Maybe, just maybe, there could be happiness waiting for her here.

With that thought, she finally closed her eyes, letting the soft whispers of the night lull her to sleep. Dreams of a possible future, tentative yet hopeful, replaced her earlier fears. She dreamed of sunlit mornings, hearty breakfasts with laughter bouncing off the walls, fields of golden wheat swaying gently in the breeze, and the touch of a man's hand not out of obligation but out of growing affection.

The dawn arrived slowly, painting the sky with hues of pink and orange. As the first rays of sunlight crept into her room, Mary awoke with a start, a newfound determination steadying her heart. Today, she would begin this new chapter. She would greet Preston with an open mind and an open heart, ready to see what life had to offer.

Slipping on her dress, she smoothed the fabric and tied her hair back. Her reflection showed a woman who, despite her insecurities, was ready to face whatever came her way. As she stepped out of her room, the aroma of freshly brewed coffee guided her to the kitchen, where Casey was already bustling about.

"Morning, Mary," Casey greeted with a warm smile. "Sleep well?"

"Well enough," Mary replied, her voice tinged with the remnants of last night's apprehensions but steadied by resolve.

"Good. There's a busy day ahead. Preston will be in soon, and then we'll see about getting you settled," Casey said, placing a reassuring hand on Mary's arm.

With a nod, Mary took a deep breath and smiled at Casey. As nervous as she was, she was ready to begin her new life as the wife of Preston Wilson.

Chapter 3

The ceremony was quick and to the point, and before she knew it, Mary and Preston were married. As they awkwardly shook hands, Casey hugged the newlyweds and left, leaving them alone as they departed the courthouse.

"Shall we go home now?" Mary asked, not knowing what to say, and suddenly felt very shy.

Preston nodded. "One stop at the Widow Jones's place. She's watching Annie for me."

For a brief moment, Mary had forgotten about Annie. An uneasy feeling crept over her as she realized she hadn't even asked who was watching the baby on her wedding day. Guilt and worry gnawed at her, overshadowing her joy. How could she have overlooked such an important detail? What type of a mother would she be?

"Widow Jones? Did she lose her husband recently?" Mary asked, waiting for Preston to help her into the wagon. Instead, she stood there while he climbed up on his side and picked up the reigns.

"What are you waiting for?" Preston asked, giving her a blank look.

Shaking her head, she pursed her lips. "Never mind," she said as she climbed up into the wagon and sat beside her new husband.

"She lost him about a year ago, and she helps me out when Annie needs watching," Preston said, turning the wagon around.

The ride to the Widow's was uneventful, with Preston pointing out certain things along the way. Having always lived near the city, Mary found the vast landscape quite impressive. Fields stretched out endlessly under the blue sky, dotted with patches of wildflowers swaying in the breeze. Mary admired the openness and undulating hills, a stark yet beautiful contrast to the bustling city streets she was used to.

Preston turned the buggy off the main road, down a small, winding lane bordered by tall, swaying grasses. "The Widow lives down here," he said.

"She lives out here all by herself?" Mary asked, wondering if Preston's house was as isolated.

"Yep. So did her Mama and Pa, and I think her grandparents, too."

As they pulled up to a small wooden house at the end of the road, Mary thought how lovely the house looked, with its neat garden and the smoke curling lazily from the chimney. She hoped her new home looked as cozy and inviting.

"Preston, I didn't expect you so soon," a young woman said, opening the door as they pulled up.

"Yes, the judge took us first thing," Preston said, jumping out of the wagon. "Widow, this here is Mary. Mary, this is the Widow Jones."

Mary nodded at the woman and smiled, pleasantly surprised. She was expecting an older lady with gray hair, not someone so young. "Very nice to meet you, Widow Jones."

"Welcome. Please call me Lenore. I'll go get Annie," the widow said as she turned and disappeared into the house, returning carrying a little bundle in her arms. "She was an angel as usual."

Handing Annie to Mary, she said, "Here you go, Annie, here's your new Ma."

Mary took the baby in her arms and gently pulled back the blanket. Annie opened one eye and looked at Mary, then grimaced as if she were objecting to the sudden interruption of her sleep. Mary looked up at Preston and smiled, her heart warming at the sight of the little girl. "She's beautiful," she said.

"Here's the rest of her things," Lenore said, handing a satchel to Preston. "Mary, if you need anything, just holler. I know things will seem a bit strange for you over the next while."

Mary nodded to the Widow, gratitude evident in her eyes. "Thank you so much. Once I get settled, you must come over for a visit."

Preston looked at the Widow and tipped his hat. "Thanks again for watching her," he said, giving the Widow a wink. "I'll be by later to finish the work."

The Widow smiled and nodded. "No rush. Get yourself settled with the new family. The work can wait," she said, giving Preston a reassuring pat on the back.

"How did her husband die?" Mary asked, looking down at the sleeping baby, her voice tinged with curiosity and empathy. "She's younger than I imagined."

Preston shook his head. "He died in an accident."

Mary nodded, absorbing the information, but couldn't help noticing the familiar ease between Preston and the Widow. She wondered why Preston hadn't married her instead of seeking a mail-order bride. Shrugging internally, she figured the reasons would reveal themselves in time.

As they pulled up in front of her new home, Mary took in the sight of the log cabin that stood before her. The front yard was nothing but dirt and stone, and in the back loomed a large barn and storage shed surrounded by endless fields. The place had a rugged charm, but she could already see where her touch would be needed to make it a home.

"This is it," Preston said, jumping down from the wagon with a tone of modest pride. "It isn't much, but it's home."

Mary smiled and gently handed Annie to him, feeling the warmth of the little girl's tiny hands as she settled into his arms. Freeing herself, Mary stepped onto the dry earth, her eyes scanning the old cabin with a glimmer of anticipation. Despite its weathered appearance, she couldn't help but imagine the treasure trove of potential that lay within these rustic walls.

The area before her was more weeds and dirt than anything else, but to Mary, it was a blank canvas, waiting for new life to be breathed into it. Off to the side, she spotted a neglected patch that appeared to have once been a thriving vegetable and flower garden. Its forgotten rows and overgrown plants told the story of a time when this place had been loved and nurtured.

With a determined nod, Mary envisioned the vibrant blooms and lush greenery she could coax back to life with some tender, loving care. She saw sweet peas, marigolds, and tomatoes flourishing in the sunlight, the garden buzzing with bees and butterflies. As she stood there, already half-lost in plans for this piece of land, Mary felt a surge of excitement. This cabin wasn't just a structure; it was a new beginning, a place where memories could be made, and roots could grow deep. She turned to him, her eyes shining with hope and possibilities, ready to transform this humble abode into a warm, welcoming home.

"Come and get yourself settled. I'll bring your trunk in later," he said, motioning her to go ahead into the house.

Opening the door, Mary took one step inside and was met with the musty scent of a place long unkempt. The floors were dusty, and cobwebs adorned the corners. She knew that if she were going to live here, cleaning would need to be her first task.

"You'll have to pardon the mess. Things have been a bit rough since Ma passed, and I just can't seem to get moving," Preston said, a note of vulnerability in his voice, as he led her to a room off the kitchen. "You can sleep in here with Annie. This is where Ma slept, at least until you get used to the place and all."

Mary followed him into the room, which had a single bed on one side and a crib on the other. The walls were bare, and the room, while simple, had a certain warmth to it.

"I was going to give you my bed, but I thought this would be better since you'll be taking care of Annie, and I want you to feel comfortable. This is, after all, your home now, too," Preston said sincerely, before handing Annie back to her and walking out of the room.

Laying Annie in her crib, Mary smiled down at the quietly sleeping baby. It was strange to think that she might be experiencing love at first sight now. Walking over to her bed, she pressed her hand into the mattress before gingerly sitting down. She took a moment to gather her thoughts, trying to come to terms with the jarring reality of her new surroundings. Her new home. Preston was a peculiar man; he didn't say much. She hoped, though, that eventually they would become familiar with each other, and the uncomfortable tension they felt now would slowly fade away.

Walking out of the bedroom, she found herself in the main area, which was divided into a sitting area, a dining table and chairs, and the kitchen. It was small but functional, with a large fireplace that seemed to be the only means of heat apart from the wood stove in the kitchen.

"Do you have running water?" Mary asked, looking around for a sink.

Preston looked at her and laughed. "If you call the pump out back running water, then yes. Things aren't as fancy around here as you're used to."

Mary smiled, appreciating his attempt at humor. "That's fine. We used to have a pump, so I know how it works. I think I'll start by cleaning this place well."

Preston nodded, a bit of relief in his eyes. "I have things to tend to in the barn," he said, quickly turning and walking out, leaving Mary standing alone.

Mary took a deep breath and looked around the room. She could see the layers of dust clinging to the surfaces, the neglected corners, and the general disarray. Yet, she also saw potential—a place where she could build a life, create a home, and perhaps find happiness.

Rolling up her sleeves, she whispered to herself, "Let's get to work." She was determined to make this house a home, one step at a time.

PRESTON WALKED OUT quickly to the barn and sat down, his mind a whirlwind of doubts and insecurities. He had no idea how to talk to a woman, let alone a lady, and Mary was definitely a lady. Casey had convinced him that getting a Mail Order Bride was a practical and promising solution, but he didn't anticipate the profound unease that now gnawed at him. Initially, the idea of having a wife seemed like a beacon of hope, a fresh start for him and little Annie. He envisioned a life of companionship, a steady, nurturing presence for his niece. But now, faced with the reality of Mary's arrival, he wasn't sure of anything. His chest tightened with every uncertain thought, the pressure growing heavier by the minute.

He didn't know what he was getting into when he signed up for a wife. He needed someone strong, someone who could work in the barn and fields alongside him. But Mary was, as they say, delicate. There was no way she could help him. She was, as his Pa used to say, small enough to blow away in the wind. Sure, she was pretty, distractingly so, but the thought of her being unable to handle the harsh reality of their life made his stomach churn. Preston felt a knot of unease tighten inside him. How would they manage?

Preston lowered himself to sit on a bale of hay, the familiar scent offering little comfort. Conversations had never been his forte. The thought of engaging Mary in meaningful dialogue felt as foreign to him as speaking a different language. He had been isolated from affectionate female interaction since his mother passed, rendering the notion of intimate conversation daunting and formidable.

Taking off his hat, he leaned against the stall, staring blankly at the wooden beams above. However, despite his fears, he couldn't ignore the undeniable attraction he'd felt when he first saw Mary. When Preston first laid eyes on her, he felt his heart skip a beat—something entirely new and thrilling. Would she be happy living here with him and Annie? Would they ever share the bond that a husband and wife are supposed to have? What if she didn't want to stay? The fear of rejection intertwined with the burden of providing for Annie, who relied on him unquestionably since her birth, compounded his anxiety.

So many worries and questions circled through the unfamiliar terrain of his emotions. Up until now, life had followed a predictable routine. He took care of Annie and managed the farm work—simple tasks, though never easy, were within his capabilities. But with Mary's arrival, his once serene existence stood at the precipice of a drastic change. This new arrangement threatened to disrupt the fragile balance he had maintained since his mother's death, and he didn't know if he was prepared for that.

MARY GLANCED UNDER the counter and spotted an old bucket. Perfect, she thought, pulling it out and heading to the pump to fill it with water. The weight of the brimming bucket was cumbersome, and she struggled to bring it back inside. Setting it on the floor with a hard thud, water splashed over the sides, spreading grime throughout the room. Watching the water turn a dirty brown, Mary shook her head in exasperation.

"What would he have done if Annie was crawling? She'd be filthy on this floor," Mary mused aloud as she scouted for extra wood for the stove. The sight of the neglected room steeled her resolve. She filled a pot with water, stoked the fire with more logs, and placed the pot to heat on the fireplace hook.

"It's going to take me a couple of pots to get this place proper," she muttered, rolling up her sleeves. If this was going to be her home, she intended to make it clean and agreeable, just like the home she had grown up in. Her mother never tolerated a dirty house, and Mary had learned those lessons well. Tidiness was more than a chore; it was a reflection of oneself, a matter of pride and self-respect.

She surveyed the room with determination burning in her eyes. "I'll have this place spic and span in no time, and if Preston doesn't like it, well, he can sleep in the barn," she said aloud, a small chuckle escaping her lips at the idea. Though the house needed attention, it had the possibility to become a warm, inviting home. Mary embraced the challenge, seeing it as a way to establish her place in this new life. She would transform this rough, neglected farmstead into a haven, just as her mother had taught her.

With renewed vigor, she began the arduous task of cleaning, her mind envisioning a bright and organized future—one where she and Preston might find some common ground and build a life together. Her practical, no-nonsense attitude clashed yet meshed with Preston's silent uncertainties, setting the stage for what was sure to be an interesting journey ahead.

Chapter 4

The next morning, Mary woke up to the fresh aroma of coffee and the sound of Annie's laughter in the other room. Getting up, she found a pitcher of water sitting on a table with a basin to wash her face and a fresh towel. After freshening up and getting dressed, she opened the door and stepped into the kitchen.

Preston, who was bouncing Annie on his knee, looked up and gave her a nod. "I made coffee. Wasn't sure if you drank it."

Mary nodded and smiled. "Thank you, I do. Do you want some breakfast," she asked.

"Don't eat breakfast, and I gave Annie her bottle. There's milk for her lunch, but you'll have to milk the cow for more milk," Preston responded, getting up and putting Annie in her cradle.

"I've never milked a cow before," Mary answered as she watched Preston reach for his hat.

"You'll figure it out," he said without looking at her. "I have to do some work in the barn and then head to the Widow's place. I'll be home for supper. There's a chicken in the icebox you might want to cook before it goes bad."

"But, could you show me how to milk the cow?" Mary asked. She had watched her grandfather once milk a cow but had never done it before. "It will just take a minute. I'm a fast learner."

"No time. I'm already late because you slept in," Preston said quickly. "I'll show you tonight."

Nodding, Mary watched as Preston opened the door and walked out, closing it behind him.

Mary stood staring at the door for a moment. She felt alone and disappointed in her husband.

"Have a nice day," she mumbled as she looked at Annie. I guess it's just you and me, Annie."

Mary spent the remainder of the morning trying to reorganize the house. Every artifact she picked up seemed to whisper stories of the past, and although she felt a pang of guilt, she knew deep down that carving out space for herself was necessary. As she worked, she found old letters obviously sent to Preston and his mother over several years from his sister. They depicted life from before—happy moments of Preston and his mother, descriptions of Annie as a newborn, and she even found a few blurry photographs of Amanda, her husband, and Annie, taken obviously after Annie was born.

Sighing, Mary had to wonder if Preston would ever be able to let go of the past.

The sun was high in the sky when Mary heard Annie's soft whimpers. Wiping her brow, she put aside the box she had been filling with trinkets and went to the cradle. Annie's small hands reached up, and Mary couldn't help but smile as she lifted her into her arms.

"Let's take a break, shall we?" Mary cooed, walking over to the window. The fields outside shimmered under the afternoon sun. It was a beautiful day, much too lovely to be spent indoors.

With Annie secured in her pram, Mary ventured out to the garden. The scent of blooming flowers and freshly turned earth was a welcome contrast to the dust she had been battling inside. Walking through the rows of vegetables and weeds, she found herself breathing easier, the open space clearing her mind.

A distant gallop caught her ear as she turned to see a figure approaching on horseback. As they drew nearer, Mary recognized it was Casey.

"Afternoon, Mary," Casey called out. "How are you settling in? Thought I'd come by and see if you needed any help."

Mary smiled, grateful for the gesture. "Afternoon, Casey. That's kind of you. Just trying to make this place feel a bit more like home."

She dismounted smoothly and walked over, her gaze falling on Annie. "Well, you look like you've got your hands full with this little one," she remarked, reaching out a finger for Annie to grab. "How is she doing?"

"She's a sweet baby. Harly any trouble at all," Mary said, her voice softening. "It's more about finding my place here."

Casey nodded. "I hear you. Preston's a good man, but he's not always the most forthcoming. Don't let that bother you too much. He needs some time to get used to the change."

Mary nodded, feeling the weight of those words. It was a sentiment she'd heard before, but it helped to know others saw it, too. "Thank you, Casey. It means a lot to hear that."

The afternoon passed pleasantly with Casey's company. She was a wealth of knowledge about the local area and shared stories about the land, the people, and even a few funny anecdotes about Preston's childhood. It made Mary feel less isolated, more connected to her new life.

As the day drew to a close, Casey took her leave, waving as she rode off towards the horizon. Mary stood at the gate, watching until she was just a speck against the setting sun. She felt a little lighter, the heavy sense of isolation lifting slightly.

Returning inside, she set about preparing supper. She seasoned the chicken from the icebox, lit a fire in the stove, and placed it in the oven. The familiar task of cooking brought a sense of normalcy, and soon, the savory aroma filled the house, mingling with the fresh scent of the flowers she had picked from the garden.

By the time Preston returned, the house had taken on a new warmth. He stepped inside, pausing to inhale deeply. "Smells good," he remarked, a faint smile playing at the corners of his mouth.

Mary looked up from setting the table. "Thank you. I thought a proper meal might be nice after a long day."

Preston nodded, glancing around the room. He noticed the changes she had made, the tidy shelves, the new arrangement of furniture. His eyes rested on a vase of wildflowers in the center of the table. "Looks like you've been busy."

"I thought it was time to start making this place our home," she said, meeting his gaze. "I hope you don't mind."

Preston shrugged. "Don't matter to me."

"I never got out to the barn to milk the cow. Would you mind doing it while I finish supper?

Without saying a word, Preston got up from the table and grabbed the pail, heading out the back door to the barn. Returning shortly with a pail full of milk, he placed it in the icebox and sat back down.

"Thank you, Preston," Mary said, putting a plate of roast chicken, roasted potatoes, and carrots in front of him.

They sat down to eat, and the silence between them was intense, each second stretching unbearably. Every small gesture—passing the bread, refilling the water glasses—seemed forced, as if they were performing an unspoken truce. Over the meal, Preston attempted to open up, sharing halting fragments about his mother, his struggles, and his hopes for Annie. Mary listened, but her heart remained guarded, every word deepening the chasm between them. She could see the hurt he carried but felt the weight of unresolved tension pressing down on them both. By the time they finished supper, she felt more uncertain than ever as to whether this was a right decision.

Although they spent a quiet evening, and Mary felt more comfortable around Preston, there was still something about him that made her feel uneasy. Their short dinner conversation had given her a glimmer of hope, and she thought she saw a different side to him, but this only seemed to amplify her concern. What was it about him that gnawed at her thoughts? Despite the pleasant moments, a pervasive sense of dread lingered, causing her to doubt her own instincts. Was she really seeing the true Preston, or was there something more sinister lurking beneath the surface?

That night, as she lay in bed, Mary stared at the ceiling, feeling the faded warmth of the day seep into her bones. There was still much to do and many bridges to build, but she no longer felt alone in the endeavor. She had Annie, a friend in Casey, and as hard as it was, she was determined to build a connection with Preston.

As she drifted off to sleep, Mary imagined the house in the years to come – filled with laughter, love, and the warmth of a family that had grown together day by day.

Chapter 5

Mary sat drumming her fingers on the table, waiting for Preston to get home. She was anxious, nervous and excited and couldn't wait to see his reaction to what she had done. She knew he would be a bit upset. After all, she did take down most of his mother's personal items, but if she wanted to make this place her own, it needed to be done. She hoped that Preston would see how much better the room looked with all the clutter gone. Now, there was lots of space for them to put the memories they would make.

The crunch of the wagon wheels outside announced that Preston was home and she put on a big smile as he walked in the door. After preparing a good meal for him, she fixed her hair and put on a clean dress. She wanted this to be the start of a great future.

"Welcome home, Preston. I trust you had a pleasant afternoon," she said happily. "I have supper all ready. I cooked the ham and made some potatoes and some peas I found growing in the garden. I hope you like it."

Preston walked in, looked at her, and nodded. "You changed your hair," he said as he hung up his hat.

"Yes. Do you like it?" she said, hoping he would approve.

"Where's Annie," Preston asked, ignoring her request for approval.

"She's still napping. I hoped we would have time for supper together before she woke up. Everything is ready," Mary said nervously, disappointed that Preston didn't say he liked her hair.

Preston scanned the room with a critical eye. "The place looks right decent. It's about time someone cleaned it up..." His voice trailed off as he stared at the blank space above the fireplace.

Mary felt her heart race uncontrollably in her chest as she watched him slowly walk over to the shelves where his mother's things had been.

"Where are my Ma's things?" he demanded, jabbing a finger at the empty mantle. "All her stuff that used to be up there. And the things on the shelves. What did you do with them?"

"Preston, I can explain," Mary replied, her voice shaky but firm.

"Explain? Explain what? Those were my Ma's belongings. You had no business touching them. They're not yours to move," Preston barked, his voice rising with each word.

"Shush, you'll wake Annie," Mary hissed. "Just let me explain."

"There's nothing to explain," Preston snapped, yanking out a chair and dropping into it. "Put them back. Now, where's my supper?"

Mary's fists clenched at her sides as she stared him down, fury bubbling inside her. How dare he shut her down like that? Did he want a wife or just a housekeeper?

"Preston Wilson, if you expect me to live here with you as your wife, you need to let me explain," Mary said, putting her hands on her hips. "I need to make this place my own. This is going to be our home."

"This is my home, and those things were my Ma's. They have been on that mantle and those shelves since I was a boy. That's where they belong," Preston said. "If you're going to live here under this roof, you'll have to obey the rules. My Ma's things aren't to be touched."

"But Preston, you told me this was my home too. Please hear .....," Mary said, trying not to sound like she was begging.

Slamming his hand down on the table, Preston sprang to his feet. "Damn it, Mary, you're my wife, and you'll do as I say! Put those things back right now. There's no room for any discussion," he bellowed, seizing his hat with a furious grip. "I've got work to do at the Widows'. I expect those things back where they belong by tomorrow or else."

Mary stood there as the door slammed shut, fighting the tears that threatened to flood her eyes. Never in her life had anyone, even her own father, spoken to her like that. Annie cried out from her crib as Mary quickly wiped her eyes and went in to get her.

"Shhhh, Annie. Did the slamming of the door wake you?" she asked as she picked up the baby and brought her to the kitchen. "It's okay, Annie."

Sitting down in the rocking chair, Mary rubbed Annie's back, trying to soothe her so she would go back to sleep. How could Preston be so thick-headed? Didn't he realize how much he had hurt her with his words?

"I guess I have to put things back," Mary said to Annie. "We certainly don't want him to get upset again."

After eating her supper alone, she put everything in the icebox and gave Annie her bottle. Once Annie had fallen back to sleep, Mary made herself a cup of tea and sat down on the chair. Preston had told her this was her house, too, and he never mentioned that certain things were off-limits.

"Maybe it was just too soon," Mary said out loud as she sipped her tea. "I'll wait a while until Preston gets used to having me around, then we'll try again."

"PRESTON, WHAT ARE YOU doing here? I didn't expect to see you again today," Lenore said gently as Preston pulled up.

Jumping out of the wagon, Preston turned and gave the Widow a weary smile. "I figured I'd get more done. The room is almost finished, and I know you're anxious."

Lenore offered a warm, understanding look as she opened the door. "I appreciate that, but I thought you'd be spending time with your new wife. You should be with her, not here working."

Preston walked into the house, his shoulders tense as he headed directly to the room he was fixing. Lenore watched him pass by, her heart going out to him, and followed quietly.

"Is there something wrong, Preston? You look troubled," Lenore said softly, leaning against the door frame.

Preston met her eyes and shook his head. "Nothing to concern you."

Lenore's voice was tender as she stepped forward. "It's your new living arrangements, isn't it?"

Preston's guarded expression faltered, and he grunted, nodding his head.

"Try to understand her side, Preston. She's a woman who's left everything familiar to move to a new place. She knows no one, and she's married a man she's never met," Lenore said, her tone soothed as she sat down on one of the storage crates. "Not only has she married a stranger, but she's with a man who's never lived with anyone other than his mother."

Preston frowned, defensive. "I'm not that hard to live with."

Lenore gave him a kind smile. "Preston, we've known each other for years, and I've visited your home a few times. I saw how your Ma used to take care of everything for you. She didn't let you lift a finger. It's natural for you to expect the same from Mary. I'm sure she is not used to living like that."

Preston opened his mouth to protest, then paused, his shoulders slowly relaxing. "I guess, in a way, I do."

Lenore's voice remained gentle. "It's an adjustment for both of you. Give it time, and try to understand what she's going through. She needs you now, more than ever."

Preston sighed and picked up his hammer. "I guess, but she is my wife. She's got to obey what I say."

Lenore put her hands on her hips and frowned. Preston, get that notion out of your head. She's your wife, not your possession. Having a happy marriage takes work from both sides."

Preston sighed. "I guess you are right. I just don't know how."

"I've not said much, but I've seen that you've had things on your mind ever since Mary arrived," Lenore said. "Plus, you've been over here working more times than you've been home."

"I guess I was kind of running from her," Preston said, looking at Lenore. "I never thought about how Mary felt."

Lenore looked at Preston and smiled. "Sometimes it takes a woman to tell a man how a woman feels. I bet Mary feels lonely and worries that maybe she made a bad decision."

"I certainly don't want her to think like that," Preston said. "She's so good with Annie; you should see how clean she's got the place looking, but she touched Ma's things. She had no right to do that."

Lenore looked at Preston. "Seems to me you need to get your priorities straight. Did you tell her not to touch those things?"

Preston shook his head. "No, I just assumed."

"So you get mad at her for doing something she didn't know she wasn't supposed to do. I wouldn't blame her if she took that next train out of here."

Preston smacked his lips and nodded. "I don't want her to leave. I have today and tomorrow left to finish up your room. I'm going to get that done, then Mary and I are going to sit down and have a talk. I think I have an apology to make."

Chapter 6

"Oh, Casey, what a great surprise," Mary cried when she opened the door later that evening. She had been sitting there fuming after Preston stormed out and needed to talk to someone. "You couldn't have come at a better time."

"Well, I was visiting my Ma, who lives up the road, and thought I'd stop by. I hope I'm not disturbing you," Casey said as she stepped inside, carefully balancing a wicker basket overflowing with ripe red strawberries. "I brought you a basket of fresh strawberries from her garden."

"Not at all, and how wonderful," Mary smiled as she took the basket, inhaling the sweet, summery scent of the fruit. For a moment, the tension in her shoulders eased.

"I know Preston loves strawberry pie. Thought maybe you could make him one," Casey nodded with a knowing smile. "You do know how to bake, don't you?"

"Oh yes. I actually love baking," Mary nodded, her voice tinged with a mix of nostalgia and frustration. "Right now, I'd rather throw a pie at Preston than bake him one."

"Oh, oh. What has Preston done this time?" Casey said, laughing lightly, trying to gauge Mary's mood.

Mary sighed deeply and motioned for Casey to sit with her at the kitchen table. The soft glow of the setting sun cast a warm light across the room, highlighting the worry lines etched across Mary's face.

"It's been a long day, Casey," Mary started, her voice low and trembling slightly. "Preston lost his temper with me for removing his mother's items. It wasn't anything drastic, just a few things here and there

"

that I thought could be put away. But he stormed off to work at the Widow's place, leaving me here... just feeling so small."

Casey's eyes widened with concern. "Mary, I'm so sorry. That must have been awful."

"I've never had any man talk to me like that, and he doesn't even realize how much he hurt me and scared me."

Casey reached across the table and took Mary's hand, squeezing it gently. "You don't deserve to be treated that way. No one does. I'll admit that Preston can be gruff sometimes but that doesn't sound like Preston."

Mary looked down at their joined hands, feeling a tear slip down her cheek. "He told me to do whatever I needed to make this place my home, and when I did, he got mad. I think sometimes he doesn't want a wife but a babysitter and a maid."

Casey nodded, understanding. "Maybe baking that pie could be a way to start a conversation, Mary. Sometimes, showing a small kindness can open the door to a bigger talk. He needs to know how you feel."

Mary took a deep breath and nodded slowly. "Maybe you're right. It's just so hard to find the right words. It seems every time I try to start a conversation with him, he shuts me down."

Casey smiled warmly. "Start with the strawberries. The rest will come. And if you need help, I'm always here."

Mary squeezed her friend's hand back, feeling a glimmer of hope. "Thank you, Casey. I don't know what I'd do without you."

Together, they sat and began to sort through the strawberries, the conversation shifting to lighter topics as the weight of the evening began to lift.

Casey shook her head. "He can be a stubborn old mule at times. Want me to talk to him?"

Mary shook her head. "No, he's my husband, and I must learn how to deal with him. As much as I respect that his mother lived here and he loved her very much, this is now my home, and I can't live there with some other woman's memories."

"I understand completely," Casey said. "Preston has been my friend for years, but there's still a lot of things about him I don't understand."

"I was terrified when he slammed his hand down on the table," Mary said. "He has to understand that he can't do that. I've never had violence in my life, and I'm certainly not going to put up with it from my husband."

Casey nodded. "A man needs to be tamed, and that's one thing that no one has ever done is tame Preston," she said, laughing. "I mean he always listened to his Ma, but that was his Ma. It's completely different now that he has a wife."

"Well, I can be just as stubborn," Mary said, throwing a strawberry into the bowl. "As much as I want to leave right now, I can't leave Annie. I really think she needs me in her life, so Preston is stuck with me."

Casey laughed. "Maybe he's met his match."

"Well, and then there's the Widow Jones," Casey said. "I still don't know why he spends so much time at her place. I know he's doing some building for her, but I've been here a week, and he's been over there every day."

Casey frowned and shook her head. "Never heard anyone say anything bad about them, but like I said, you need to talk to Preston about that one. It's not my place to tell you what happened."

"Am I wrong for worrying like I do?" Mary asked. "I sometimes feel I should just be thankful that he has given me a place to live."

"No, Mary. That's not what your coming here was all about. Preston put the ad in for a Mail Order Bride because he wanted companionship and love and to make a family for Annie. I know he's a good man, and I know he would make a good husband. He just needs time to understand what it's all about."

Mary looked at Casey. "I'm bound and determined to make this work, too. I have nothing for me back home. Preston and Annie are my home now, and I'm willing to be as patient as I need to be, but I won't put up with an outburst like he did. Am I wrong in my feeling?"

Casey looked at her new friend. "No, you are right to feel the way you do and it's wrong for Preston to be acting like a dang fool."

"Thanks, Casey. I knew I could count on you," Mary said, smiled.

"Well, I should get going," Casey said. "Looks like you have enough strawberries to make two pies. One to eat and one to throw."

Mary laughed. "I just might do that."

After Casey left, Mary put the chucked strawberries into the icebox and tidied the table. Annie stirred in her cradle, and Mary realized it was time to change and get her ready for bed. Casey's words kept playing over and over in her head. Will Preston come around? Would he wake up one day and see things from Mary's point of view? Could she wait around for it to happen? Would they ever be a happy family?

After giving Annie her last bottle of the night, she rocked her to sleep, hoping Preston would come in and apologize for his outburst. Casey had said he was a kind and patient man, but so far, Mary saw a pig-headed cowboy who wasn't willing to budge.

Once Annie had fallen asleep, Mary lit a few lamps and sat in the rocking chair to think. What would she do if this marriage didn't work out? Could she leave? She had fallen in love with Annie and couldn't bear the thought of not having her in her life. If she stayed, could she eventually learn to love Preston? Before too long, she felt herself dozing off and decided to go ahead and go to bed. She had no idea when Preston would be home, and as far as she was concerned, he didn't deserve her waiting up for him.

As she lay in her bed in the dark, she heard the sound of Preston coming into the house, which made the butterflies in her stomach flutter even more than they were. Laying with her back towards her door, she heard Preston gently open her bedroom door.

"Are you awake, Mary?" he whispered in the dark.

Mary stared silently at the wall, deciding if she should say anything. Was he reaching out to her? Should she get up and talk to him?

After a moment of silence, she heard the soft click of the door as Preston shut it. Mary turned and looked toward the door. Had she missed her chance? Should she have said something? Her mind was in turmoil. Mary lay in the dark for a while, thinking about what she should do. Casey had been right; they weren't going to settle anything if they didn't talk, but was tonight the right time? Mary was still angry with his outburst and hurt with his behavior. She could hear him moving around in the main room, and despite her desire to talk to him, she decided to stay in bed. If they were going to talk about anything, they both needed to be calm, and right now Mary didn't trust her feelings.

She thought of her beautiful house that she had grown up in and was once so happy in, picking flowers with her mother in her garden and laughing with her father as he chased her around the yard and how every Sunday morning, her mother would make a big breakfast after they got home from Church. Those were the memories she had and the type of memories she wanted to create with her own family.

In a way, she could understand his reluctance of getting rid of his mother's things, but he needed to know where she stood and how she felt. Casey kept saying he was a kind man, and hopefully in a few days when they talked, she would be able to see that side of him and begin creating a life together, based on honesty, respect and hopefully one day, love.

Her parents always taught her that if she made a promise or a commitment, she must follow through regardless of the outcome. She had made a commitment to Preston to be his wife, and she was going to follow through. If Preston was the type of man that Casey kept saying he was, eventually he would come around. It was going to take a lot of hard work and prayer, but Mary was bound and determined that her marriage was going to be a happy one especially for Annie's sake.

Chapter 7

The next morning, Mary awoke to the relentless howling of the wind battering the walls of their modest cabin. With a sinking feeling, she noticed that Annie's crib was empty. Knowing Preston must be up and about, she dreaded facing him after their heated argument the previous day. She quickly dressed, steeling herself for the inevitable encounter, and made her way to the kitchen area.

"Morning," Preston greeted, sipping his coffee at the table. "Annie was awake early, so I didn't want her to disturb you."

Mary forced a smile, grateful for the small gesture. "Thank you, Preston. I didn't sleep very well last night," she admitted, pouring herself a cup of coffee.

As she sat down at the worn oak table across from Preston, she opened her mouth to speak, but before she could utter a word, a powerful gust of wind blew the front door open with a loud crash.

"Dang. I keep meaning to fix that," Preston muttered, jumping up to secure the door. "When the wind picks up like this, you have to remember to put the latch on."

Mary glanced out the window, anxiety gnawing at her. "Sounds like a storm is coming."

"Yep, we get some mean ones around here," Preston replied, resuming his seat. "I suppose you aren't used to these winds."

Mary shook her head, her unease growing with each passing second. "No, we had thunder and lightning back home, but not winds like this."

Preston leaned back in his chair, an understanding look in his eyes. "Well, latch the door after I leave, and you should be okay."

Mary's heart skipped a beat. "You aren't leaving me?" she asked, her voice trembling.

"I got work to finish at the Widow's place. It's just going to take a few hours, and I'll be home," Preston said gently but firmly. "Then I'm hoping you and I can sit down and talk. We need to settle some things."

"Preston, I'm scared. I hate storms, and the wind is terrifying," Mary confessed, her fear palpable. "Please stay home."

Preston's face softened, but his resolve did not waver. "Sorry, Mary. I promised the Widow I'd be by. Latch the door, and you'll be fine." He rose to leave, taking his hat off the wall hook, as the wind howled outside. The moment he opened the door, the wind wrenched it from his grasp, slamming it against the wall with a deafening bang.

Mary jumped, her eyes wide with fear as she looked outside. Dirt and debris swirled around the yard in a chaotic dance. "You surely aren't taking the buggy out in this?" she exclaimed.

"I'm just bringing the horse. It'll be quicker. They're used to this weather," Preston reassured her, his voice steady. "Latch the door." With that, he stepped out into the storm, the door crashing shut behind him.

Mary wasted no time in securing the latch, her heart pounding in her chest. How could he leave her alone? She felt abandoned, petrified by the ferocity of the storm. Was the Widow more important than keeping his wife and child safe?

The cabin was under siege from the elements. The wind howled like a wild beast, and soon, rain began to pelt against the windows with such force that Mary feared they would shatter. Peering outside, she could see nothing but a wall of white as the torrential downpour obscured everything. The cabin's wooden structure creaked and groaned under the onslaught, and Mary knew they were in grave danger.

Annie's cries pierced through the roar of the wind. Mary rushed to her cradle, scooping her up and cradling her close. Desperation set in as she searched for a safe place to hide. The sturdy table in the kitchen seemed like the best option.

"The table," Mary muttered to herself, grabbing a few blankets before crawling underneath with Annie. "Annie, we're going to be okay. Shush, sweet baby, it's going to be okay."

The wind roared louder, rattling the walls and windows. Mary clutched Annie tightly, her heart racing as the cabin seemed to shake to its very foundations. Suddenly, with a thunderous crash, the roof was torn away, exposing them to the fury of the storm.

"Pressssstooooon," Mary screamed, her voice barely audible over the deafening noise. Her cry was cut short as a massive tree toppled, smashing through the cabin and collapsing the table above her and Annie.

In an instant, everything went dark. The wind continued to howl, but Mary could no longer hear it. The weight of the table trapped her, and she held onto Annie with all her strength as consciousness slipped away. Her last thoughts were filled with a desperate hope that Preston would come back for them.

"PRESTON, WHAT ON EARTH are you doing here?" Lenore said, her brow furrowed in concern as she opened the door. "You should be home, you know that. This weather isn't fit to be out in."

"I've got a few more hours left of work on the room, and I want to get it done," Preston replied, stepping inside and shaking off the drizzle clinging to his coat.

"How's Mary?" Lenore asked. "She must be terrified. I'm sure she's never seen winds like this."

Preston shrugged, though a flicker of worry passed over his face. "A bit, but she'll be fine. I told her to latch the door and just stay inside."

They moved into the room where Preston had been working, and he picked up his tools to finish putting the last planks on the walls. Every strike of the hammer echoed his doubts, his mind replaying the fearful look Mary gave him as he'd walked out earlier. Maybe he should have stayed, but he convinced himself she needed to get used to these storms if she was going to live here.

"Preston, I don't think this is an ordinary thunderstorm," Lenore said, her voice suddenly urgent as she burst into the room. "It's as dark as night over your way."

Preston dropped his hammer and rushed to the window. His heart sank. "That's a tornado," he exclaimed, his voice trembling.

"A tornado?" Lenore echoed, her eyes widening in shock as she joined him at the window. Together, they watched in horror as the funnel cloud touched down and began its relentless path toward his home. "Preston, that looks like it's right over your house."

"Mary and Annie," Preston cried out, his voice breaking. "I've got to go."

"Preston, you can't go out in this," Lenore cried after him, but her words fell on deaf ears.

He bolted out of the house, running to the barn where his horse was tied. Frantically untying the reins, he leapt onto the horse's back. "Come on. We have to get home," he urged, nudging the horse into a gallop.

The horse galloped down the road, and Preston's eyes remained locked on the voracious funnel cloud. Debris was already swirling around it, and he whispered desperate prayers that his house—and his family—would be spared.

"WHOA!" he cried, yanking the reins as the tornado suddenly changed direction, bearing down on the road ahead. He veered off into a field, urging the horse faster, wild with fear that the tornado would reach his home before he did.

But as quickly as it had descended, the tornado lifted back into the clouds, leaving a trail of destruction in its wake. A wet drizzle fell as Preston guided the horse back to the main road. His heart pounded louder with every step; barns, fences, and trees lay scattered like discarded toys, deepening his dread. It seemed more and more likely that the tornado had torn through his property.

The road to his house was impassable, choked with debris so thick he had to dismount and lead the horse on foot. Holding his breath, he rounded the final bend, his worst fears realized as he took in the chaotic pile of logs, trees, and shattered planks that had once been his home.

"Mary! Annie!" he cried out, voice raw with grief. "I'm so sorry. So, so very sorry." Blind with tears, he began clawing at the wreckage, throwing aside planks and branches. "I should have listened to you. I should have stayed," he repeated over and over, desperate for a miracle. "Please, God, let them be okay. Please."

His hands bled from splinters and rough wood, but he didn't stop. Suddenly, his eyes caught a glimpse of fabric beneath a board. Heart pounding, he pulled it free and his world stopped. It was a small shoe, the same type Annie wore. Bloodstained.

His breath left him in a strangled sob, tears streaming down his face. This couldn't be happening. He dropped to his knees, clutching the tiny shoe to his chest, the weight of his sorrow almost unbearable.

Chapter 8

"**O**h, Annie. My sweet, sweet Annie," he whimpered, holding the tiny shoe to his chest as if it were a talisman. His eyes darted heavenward, wild with desperation. "Why God. Why?"

Distant shouts of neighbors echoed through the chaos, each shout amplifying his terror.

Frantically lifting another board, his hands trembled as he glimpsed something white amid the rubble. He tore at the debris with feverish haste.

"No, no, Mary!" he screamed, the sight of her hand protruding from beneath the collapsed table striking him with raw fear. A log from the crushed roof pinned the tabletop down, and Mary's motionless hand was his only sign of her presence.

Preston's heart pounded as he struggled to lift the weight. His frantic eyes searched for help.

"Preston, is everything alright?" Joe Millar called out, his buggy creaking ominously. "We're checking in on everyone. Looks like your place got the worse of it."

"Joe, help me! Mary and Annie—they're trapped! I can't get them out!" Preston's voice cracked with panic. "I need something to pry this log off!"

Jumping off his horse, Joe grabbed a plank and a rock. Together, the two men labored with trembling hands, prying the log with desperate strength. Every second felt like an eternity, each creak of the wood a thunderclap in their ears.

Finally, they heaved the table away. Preston's breath caught in his throat as he gazed upon Mary's bloodied, unconscious form. Half her face was obscured in a mask of red, a terrifying reminder of the fragile line between life and death.

"Mary, I'm so sorry. So very sorry," Preston chanted in a voice thick with terror. Beneath her, Annie wailed loudly, her cry piercing through the night like a distress signal, amplifying the dread rooted deep in Preston's soul.

"Annie, my sweet baby!" Preston's voice cracked with fear as he scooped her up, realizing Mary had shielded her with her own body, absorbing the brunt of the impact.

"Preston, is she okay?" Joe Millar's voice trembled.

"Annie's fine, but Mary's hurt bad," Preston's hands shook. "She needs to get to the Doctor. Now."

"Where's Preston?" Lenore's frantic voice cut through the chaos. "Preston, where are Marie and the baby?"

"Over here, Widow. I need to get Mary to the Doctor!" Preston's voice was desperate as he handed Annie to Lenore. "Can you take care of her? Mary protected her."

"How's Mary?" Lenore's concern was palpable.

"Hurt pretty bad, from what I can tell." Preston's eyes welled up as he lifted Mary's limp, bloodied body.

"I've got my buggy. The Doctor has set up a small hospital at his house to care for the injured," Joe urged, guiding Preston through the debris to his waiting buggy.

"Go, Preston. Don't worry about Annie. I'll take her home," Lenore said, her grip on the sobbing baby tightening. "Go take care of your wife."

The drive to the hospital felt like an eternity, with roads blocked by fallen trees. Finally, they arrived. Jumping out, Preston carefully lifted Mary from the back of the wagon, sprinting into Doc Haywood's office.

"Help! I need the doctor!" His voice was a mix of fear and urgency.

The office was chaotic as people with various injuries sat around, waiting their turn.

"Put her here," a nurse directed, patting an empty cot off to the side. "Doc Haywood is just finishing up with someone."

Preston laid Mary down, gripping her hand, tears streaming down his cheeks. He gently stroked her face, kissing her forehead.

The nurse returned with a basin, tenderly cleaning the blood from Mary's face. "Just a small cut and a nasty bump. The doctor will be with her soon."

"Where am I?" Mary's voice was weak as her eyes fluttered open.

"Shh, you're at the Doctor's office. You've had a bad hit, but I'm here," Preston reassured, his voice shaking.

"Annie, where's Annie?" Panic surged in Mary's voice as she tried to sit up.

"Mary, be still. Annie's fine. You protected her. She's okay, but you need to rest," he implored.

Mary looked at him, then slumped back, exhaustion overtaking her.

"Preston, what's the situation?" Doc Haywood approached the bed.

"Doc, she was hit on the head during the tornado. I found her unconscious," Preston's desperation was evident. "The tornado went right through my place."

Doc Haywood examined Mary while Preston clung to her hand. "She's going to be fine. She's lucky. It's just couple of cuts and a bump to the head. Keep an eye on her, and if she shows any serious symptoms, bring her back," Doc Haywood instructed. "She is gonna need rest in bed for a few days."

Preston nodded, relief washing over him. "Thank you, Doctor. Our home is gone. The tornado destroyed it."

"I'm sure there are places offering shelter," Doctor Wells offered.

"Thanks, Doc. We'll manage," Preston said as he gently helped Mary sit up. "I know where we can go."

Gently putting Mary in the wagon, Preston climbed up beside her, cradling her against him. If anything happened to her, he would never forgive himself.

A slight moan escaped Mary's lips as she opened her eyes slightly and looked up at her husband. "Preston, what are we going to do? Our home?" Mary's voice broke, and her hand felt a bump on her head.

"We'll go to Lenore's. She's watching Annie," Preston assured her, helping her to the wagon. "We'll start over."

The name Lenore struck Mary like a sudden shiver, making her flinch involuntarily. She couldn't grasp the reason, but the name wrapped around her in a cloak of unease. Unable to muster even the slightest bit of strength, she let her head sink back down. She was too exhausted to resist, too weary to care.

As they arrived at Lenore's, Preston carried Mary's sleeping form out of the wagon.

"Thanks, Joe. I appreciate it," Preston said, shaking Joe's hand. "I need to check on the cows in the barn."

"It looks like the barn wasn't touched. I'll check your place," Joe offered. "You just tend to your family."

Lenore rushed out the door. "Mary, Preston, I was so worried. Come inside."

Preston carried Mary into the kitchen. "The doctor said she'll be fine. She just needs rest."

"I've got a room ready upstairs. You'll stay with me until you rebuild," Lenore said, putting on the kettle. "Annie's asleep."

"We can't impose," Preston hesitated.

"Nonsense. We're neighbors and friends." Lenore smiled. "Company will be good. Go get Mary settled in bed upstairs."

"Where's Preston? Annie? Mary?" Carey shouted, exploding through the door. "I saw their place. It's completely gone."

Lenore's smile was a stark contrast. "Preston is getting Mary settled in the spare room, and Annie is sleeping. I just made some tea. How did you fare?"

"Dang thing missed my place by a few miles, but I watched it tear right through Preston's house. Jumped on my horse as soon as it was clear. Joe told me he brought them here. Are they alright?"

"Preston is fine. He was here when the tornado struck. Annie is okay, thanks to Mary. She took the worst of it," Lenore said, her smile unwavering. "Thank God no one was killed."

"What do you mean Preston was here?" Carey's voice bristled with confusion.

"He came to finish his work. I told him he should be home but he insisted."

"That damn fool," Casey growled. "He's getting an earful from me when I see him. I gotta go. I told Doc Haywood I'd lend a hand. Lots of injuries. Tell Preston I'll be back."

Lenore nodded, her smiled never fading. "You're a good friend to him, Casey. He always speaks highly of you."

"Well, after I'm done with him, he might think differently," Casey muttered, the words laced with both frustration and relief.

Chapter 9

Opening her eyes, Mary blinked rapidly, trying to make sense of her surroundings, her gaze settling on the gingham curtains swaying slightly in the breeze. Groggily lifting her head off the pillow, she spotted the Widow Jones dozing in a chair in the corner.

"Where am I?" she whispered, the words shaky and uncertain.

At the sound of Mary's voice, the Widow startled awake and quickly moved to the bedside. "You're at my place, Mary. Safe and sound."

A rush of panic surged through Mary. "Where's Annie? I need to find Annie!"

"It's okay. Annie is fine. She's tucked away in a cradle, sound asleep. You, Annie, and Preston are going to stay with me until you can rebuild," the Widow reassured, pressing a cool glass of water to Mary's lips. "Here, take a sip. Everyone is safe."

Mary's mind raced as she struggled to push herself upright. "I should get up. There's so much to do."

"Oh no, you don't," the Widow said gently but firmly, easing Mary back against the pillows. "Doc Haywood gave strict orders for you to be on bed rest for a few days. You took a nasty bump to the head. Do you remember any of it?"

Mary lay back, her thoughts swirling chaotically. "I remember... the wind, grabbing Annie, but then everything gets fuzzy, like I was walking through a dense fog."

"The Doctor insists on bed rest until you regain your strength," Lenore said, her tone compassionate yet authoritative. "Annie is depending on your getting better."

Without much resistance, Mary sank back into the pillows, her eyes fluttering shut. "I think I'll sleep a bit longer if that's alright."

"Of course, Mary. Rest as much as you need. I'll be downstairs if you need anything," the Widow said softly, retreating from the room.

As Mary drifted back to sleep, a confused haze clouded her thoughts. She may not recall all the events clearly, but she remembered enough to feel a knot of frustration tightening in her chest. If Preston hadn't been at the Widow's place fixing her room, Mary and Annie wouldn't have had to face the tornado alone. Despite the feelings of anger she had towards the Widow, she appreciated her hospitality.

PRESTON CAME INTO THE Widow's kitchen and slumped down on a chair, looking at the Widow as she prepared a tray of food. His face was a portrait of frustration and weariness, his fingers tangling through his hair in a restless motion.

"How's Mary," he muttered, barely above a whisper.

"She's sleeping now," the Widow replied gently. "I'm getting this tray ready for her when she wakes. She needs to start eating if she's gonna get her strength back."

"I went over to the house to survey the damage. The house is completely gone," Preston said, his voice tight with anger and disbelief. "All that's left is the foundation. I found a few items among the rubble, but we've pretty much lost everything. I made such a fuss about Mary taking down all of Ma's things, and now, after the storm, I'd be lucky if I can find one thing."

Lenore looked at Preston and smiled sympathetically. "Funny how things work out. I have to ride into town; can you keep an eye on Annie and check on Mary? If she wakes, you can give her this tray."

Preston nodded, his gratitude tinged with frustration. "Really appreciate you letting us stay here, Widow. I don't know what we'd do without you."

"What are friends for," Lenore said with a smile as she walked out the door.

Preston took a deep breath, trying to push down the anger gnawing at his insides, and peeked in on Annie, who was still asleep in her cradle. Tiptoeing upstairs, he went into Mary's room and looked down at her, sleeping fitfully. Reaching out, he stroked her cheek, his anger momentarily giving way to a lump of sorrow in his throat.

"Preston, is that you?" Mary said groggily, her voice a fragile whisper.

"Yes, Mary. It's me. Are you hungry or want anything," Preston said, sitting on the bed and taking her hand. "The Widow prepared a tray for you."

Mary shook her head. "I need water," she said, licking her dry lips.

Preston jumped up and grabbed the glass of water that was sitting on the nightstand. "Mary, I'm so sorry this happened."

Mary took a sip of water, then looked at Preston with eyes clouded by anger and hurt. "I begged you not to go."

"Yes, I know, and I can't tell you how sorry I am that I didn't listen to you," Preston said, his voice cracking as he sat on the side of the bed.

"I begged you to stay because I was scared," Mary said, scowling as she tried to remember the events of the past few days. "There was a storm."

"Yes, that's right," Preston said, his frustration bubbling close to the surface. "I feel really bad too."

"I wanted you to stay and protect Annie and me, but you felt it was more important to come to the Widow's to work," Mary said, sitting up slightly, her anger sharpening with each word.

"Mary, please. Don't get upset. Lay back down."

"No, I remember it all now. I pleaded with you to stay, and you told me no," Mary said, her anger erupting. "You told me you had to come here and that all I needed to do was lock the door."

Preston hung his head, the weight of his mistake pressing down on him, mixed with the burning anger at the unjust twist of fate.

"Mary, please. Don't get upset," Preston said, his voice tinged with desperation. "I'm so sorry I upset you."

"Preston," Mary replied, sitting up completely, her mind suddenly becoming clear. "If we want this relationship to work, some changes must be made. I came here because I thought you wanted a wife to share a loving relationship with and make a life. But you just want a maid, and I won't do that. As much as I love Annie, I love myself even more, and I won't be mistreated or spoken to the way you did," Mary said, locking eyes with him. "When your wife needed you the most, you left her to work for another woman."

"I've hurt you so much," Preston said, his voice breaking as he grasped the depth of her pain.

"I really appreciate Lenore letting us stay here, but since we arrived, you've spent more time with her than with me," Mary said, her frustration evident. "Maybe I had no right taking your mother's things down, but I was just trying to make it our place. You had no right to get angry at me the way you did."

Preston nodded his head, regret washing over him. "I know that now, Mary. I shouldn't have lost my temper. I'm not used to having a wife, and I didn't think. But it all doesn't matter anymore."

"What do you mean?" Mary asked, her frustration giving way to concern. "It doesn't matter."

"My Ma's things are all lost. The house is completely demolished, and everything is gone," Preston confessed, shoulders slumping.

Mary looked at him, the fight draining out of her. "What are we going to do?"

"Mary, I want you to just get better. Try not to think about the past few days. Let's move on, rebuild the house, and make it our home," Preston said, his tone pleaded. "That is if you can forgive me."

Mary looked at Preston, her eyes softening despite the residual hurt. "Annie is okay?"

"Yes, she's fine. You saved her. You took the brunt of the tree when it fell. That's what saved Annie," Preston said. "Get some rest. I'll bring her to see you before she goes to bed tonight."

As he walked out of Mary's room, he was met with a surprise. The Widow stood outside the door, her expression grim.

"Preston, you and I need to talk," Lenore said, scowling. "I didn't mean to eavesdrop, but I'm certainly glad I did."

Chapter 10

"**I**s what Mary said true?" Lenore's voice held a mix of concern and disapproval as she confronted Preston in the cozy warmth of the kitchen. The scent of freshly baked bread hung in the air, a stark contrast to the tension that had accompanied them into the room.

Preston met her gaze, his eyes reflecting a turmoil he could no longer hide. "Pretty much," he admitted after a pause that felt like an eternity.

"Preston Wilson, I've known you for several years, and I never pegged you for a man who would shirk his responsibilities. If you didn't want a wife, why on earth did you send for one?" Lenore's tone was firm, but there was an underlying note of compassion that softened her lecture.

Preston sighed deeply, lowering himself into a chair at the worn wooden table. "Casey was the one who suggested it. She felt I needed a wife."

Lenore pursed her lips thoughtfully. "Well, I certainly won't argue with her. Did you agree with her?"

"At the time, I did," Preston confessed, running a hand through his hair in a gesture of frustration. "But after Mary arrived, I got scared and felt I had made a mistake. I figured she would be shy and quiet and just do as I told her. Instead, she had a mind of her own. It wasn't until I almost lost her that I realized how much I had come to love her."

Compassion filled Lenore's eyes as she took a seat beside him, placing her hands over his in a comforting gesture. "Preston, it's okay to be scared. You've had a lot of change in your life recently, but I think Mary is the best thing to ever happen to you, especially for Annie."

Preston nodded, tears shimmering in his eyes. "You're right, Widow. I feel so bad for everything that happened."

"Look, I like Mary, but if your daily visits here have put a strain on your relationship, then that's just not right," Lenore said, her arms crossing over her chest in a protective stance. "I won't be the cause of trouble in your marriage."

"I'll explain everything to her when she is better," Preston said, determination creeping into his voice.

"You've never told her anything about James, have you?" Lenore's question hung heavy in the air.

Preston's head dropped lower. "No, I never did. I guess I'm a failure as a husband. Mary is too good for me."

"Now, now," Lenore soothed, patting his hand. "Don't put yourself down. I think the best thing we can do is go talk to Mary and explain a few things to her. Maybe when she hears the whole story, she'll understand."

"I HAVE SOMEONE I THINK you'll want to see," Preston said a few days later as he poked his head into Mary's room, his smile hesitant but hopeful.

Mary sat up, eyes brightening at the sight of him. "Just what I need right now," she said happily, her voice a balm to his troubled heart.

Preston entered the room holding Annie, who squealed with delight at the sight of her. As he carefully handed the baby to Mary, he sat tenderly on the edge of the bed, and with a reassuring nod, Lenore pulled up a chair closer.

"Hey Annie," Mary cooed, her fingers gently stroking the baby's soft curls. "Did you miss me?"

Annie nestled against Mary, her tiny frame relaxing as if finding peace in her arms.

Mary looked from Preston to Lenore, sensing the significance of their presence. "You both look like you have something to say."

"We do, Mary," Lenore began, her voice steady. "I think you need an explanation, something Preston should have talked to you about when you first came here."

"About what?" Mary's curiosity was tinged with apprehension, as if unsure whether she wanted to hear the truth.

"About us. Preston and I. I overheard you talking to him the other day," Lenore said, an apologetic look on her face. "First of all, I wasn't being nosy. I came back to the house to get something, and the door was partly open. I heard everything."

"Mary, it's not what you think," Preston said quickly. "I don't want to lose you."

Lenore leaned forward, placing a warm hand on Mary's arm. "Mary, I was married to my husband, James, for four wonderful years. We had great dreams, and we were very much in love."

"The widow's husband worked with me down at the sawmill. We became really good friends, and I knew the Widow already," Preston added, his voice tinged with past fondness and present sorrow.

"Preston and I went to school together, but me being younger, we didn't really know each other, and as we got older, we became friends," Lenore picked up the tale. "I met James when he came into town looking for work. My Pa hired him to do some work on our farm, and we fell in love, and he decided to stay."

"I bumped into Lenore one day in town, and she told me about James and how he wanted to find work. I knew they were looking at the sawmill, so I got him the job," Preston continued. "We became instant friends, and he helped build my barn when I decided to try my hand at ranching. We were going to do it together. We had big plans to leave the sawmill and get into cattle ranching."

Mary's eyes widened in surprise. "I didn't realize you used to work in the sawmill."

"It's not something I like to talk about, but you'll see why in a minute," Preston said. "The barn was built, and I had purchased a few head of cattle. I promised my boss I would work one more week at the sawmill. On my last day, James and I were cutting the last few planks of the day when one of the saws jammed. I told James to hold on, and I'd go and get the pry bar so we could unjam it. As I turned and walked away, I heard a noise, but I kept on walking, grabbed the pry bar and as I came around I saw James. He had tried to free the sawblade himself by kicking it. His foot got trapped against the winch and the log, and he was trying desperately to free himself as the log inched closer to the saw," Preston recounted, his voice breaking, his eyes filled with unshed tears.

"Preston, I had no idea," Mary said, her hand finding his, offering silent support.

"By the time I ran to the main switch, it was too late," Preston whispered, the weight of the memory pressing down on him. "I managed to free him, pulled him out, and he died in my arms. He died because of me because I wasn't fast enough."

Mary, tears streaming down her face, squeezed Preston's hand tighter. "I'm so sorry."

"Preston has been dealing with tremendous guilt, even if I've tried to convince him it wasn't his fault," Lenore explained gently. "That's why he does a lot of work around my place. It's all things that James left unfinished. There is nothing between Preston and me except that we mourn the same man."

"I feel so stupid for thinking the worst," Mary said, wiping her cheeks.

"You had no way of knowing, my dear," Lenore reassured her, a motherly smile on her lips. "It happened a year ago, and we have slowly been trying to move on."

"I should have explained it to you when you got here," Preston confessed, his voice laced with regret. "And I should have been a better husband and talked to you proper. Mary, I'm sorry for causing you so much upset."

Mary smiled through her tears. "Now that I understand, it all feels so different. I'm so sorry, Lenore, for thinking the way I did."

"Understandable, my dear," Lenore said as she stood up, patting Preston's shoulder. "I'm going to go down and make us all a nice dinner. I think you could use some real food other than soup or broth."

Mary's smile widened as Lenore left the room. Turning to Preston, she shook her head slightly. "I'm sorry for everything."

"You don't have anything to apologize for. I need lessons on how to be a good husband," Preston admitted, his sincerity clear. "I'm sorry. When I thought you had died, I thought my life was over."

"Well, I didn't die," Mary said, a playful glint in her eyes. "I guess you're stuck with me."

"Mary, I don't know anything about love or being a husband. I'm just a country boy who grew up in a small town. I don't have much education, and I don't know if I'm gonna be any good at ranching," Preston said, his voice earnest. "But I sure as heck am gonna try and work really hard to be everything you want me to be."

Mary looked at him, her heart swelling with affection. "Well, let's start over," she said, extending her hand. "Hello Mr. Wilson, my name is Mary Johnson, and I'm here to be your wife."

Preston took her hand, a new sense of hope and determination blooming in his chest. "It's a pleasure to meet you, Miss Johnson. I promise I'll do my best to make you happy."

As the couple sat there, holding hands and sharing newfound understanding, a sense of peace settled over them, signaling the beginning of a new chapter in their lives.

Chapter 11

"How soon will you be able to start building again?" Mary asked one evening as she was preparing for bed. She and Preston had made it a habit to sit together in her room in the evenings and talk. It was their way of starting over and getting to know each other.

"Well, I figure next week, I can start cleaning up the mess and check on the floor," Preston replied, his voice steady and reassured. "I think we may be able to just rebuild the walls and roof and use some of the existing logs if they aren't too damaged. Once we start building, it should go fast."

Mary nodded, her fingers fiddling with the hem of her nightgown. "As much as I enjoy having Lenore to talk to, and I appreciate everything she has done for us," she said, "I'll be happy to get into my own home."

Preston chuckled, a warmth spreading through his chest at her words. "Can't argue with you there," he said, smiled.

"I'm glad the cows are okay," Mary said, sitting on the side of the bed. "I guess it's a blessing that they were all in the barn."

Preston couldn't help but laugh. "We refer to them as cattle, and no, thank the good Lord, everything was fine."

Mary stuck her tongue out at her husband playfully. "You'll have to educate me on the ways of ranching."

"Are you ready to be a rancher's wife?" Preston asked, smiled at her, a teasing glint in his eye. "You may have to come out to the barn sometimes to help birth, bale hay, stuff like that."

Mary chuckled. "I think I can handle that. Everything has been an adventure since I've come here, and I'm not afraid to get my hands dirty."

"Mary, we are going to have a great life," Preston said, leaning forward from the chair he was sitting on in the corner of the bedroom. "You, Annie, and I... I'm hoping we can start our own family eventually."

Mary looked at Preston, her heart fluttering. In the past few weeks, she had seen the real side of Preston Wilson—the side that she had fallen deeply in love with. This was the man she wanted to spend her life with.

"Well, I think I'm going to turn in now," Preston said, getting up from his chair. He had been sleeping on a small cot that Lenore had set up in the sitting room, giving Mary the bedroom while she recuperated. He didn't want her to feel uncomfortable or rush her into anything. Going over to Mary, he looked at her and smiled. "You are the prettiest little thing I have ever seen. I still can't believe you traveled all that way to be my wife."

Mary looked at him and blushed. "I'm glad I came here too. I never thought I would be happy, but I really am. It's sad to think it took a tornado to knock some sense into both of us."

Preston laughed, his eyes crinkling at the corners. "Well, I'll let you go to sleep. Goodnight, Mary," Preston said as he turned to go downstairs.

Mary gently caught his arm, causing him to turn and gaze into her eyes. "Please stay," she whispered, her voice soft and tender. With Lenore away for the week visiting her sister, they finally had the perfect opportunity to embrace their moments together and truly become man and wife.

"Are you sure, Mary?" Preston said, facing her, his heart pounding. "It's not too soon? I don't want to hurt you."

Mary looked at him, putting her hand against his cheek, her touch soft and reassuring. "I think it's time. Close the door."

Preston stood still for a moment, searching her eyes. Seeing the love and trust there, he nodded. He gently closed the door, enclosing them in the cocoon of the dimly lit room. The flickering candle cast long shadows, creating an intimate, velvety darkness around them.

He moved closer to her, taking a seat on the edge of the bed. Mary reached out, her hands trembling slightly, and took his hand in hers.

They sat like that for a moment, enveloped in a comfortable silence that spoke volumes more than words ever could.

"I've waited so long to feel this close to you," Mary whispered, her eyes glistening with unshed tears of happiness. "I was afraid of losing you even before I had the chance to truly know you."

Preston's grip on her hand tightened slightly, his other hand coming up to brush a stray lock of hair from her face. "You'll never lose me, Mary," he said softly. "I'm here, and I plan to stay."

He reached out to gently pull her into his arms. Mary went willingly, resting her head against his chest, listening to the steady beat of his heart. They held each other for a long moment, the world outside the room feeling distant and unimportant.

"I promise to always take care of you," Preston murmured into her hair. "To build us a home where we can be happy and safe."

Mary pulled back slightly to look into his eyes. "And I promise to be by your side, through everything. To learn and grow with you."

Preston smiled, his heart swelling with love and gratitude. He leaned down to kiss her softly, sealing their unspoken vows.

They slowly lay down together, the bed creaking softly under their combined weight. Mary nestled close, feeling Preston's warmth and security envelop her. For the first time in a long while, she felt truly at peace.

"I don't have much experience," Preston confessed, his voice barely a whisper as he gazed into her eyes, captivated by their depth and beauty.

Mary's cheeks flushed a delicate pink, and she returned his smile with a gentle, tender one of her own. "Neither do I, Preston," she murmured softly, her voice carrying a sweet promise. "I guess we will learn together."

As the candle continued to flicker, casting a gentle glow over the room, Mary closed her eyes, contentment filling her. She knew that whatever challenges lay ahead, they would face them together—stronger and more united than ever before.

And in that quiet, shared intimacy, the foundations of their future were laid, not with bricks and mortar, but with love and trust, ready to weather any storm.

Chapter 12

"Today is the day!" Preston exclaimed to Mary as soon as she returned from changing Annie.

"What do you mean?" Mary asked, her curiosity piqued as she gently set Annie on the small blanket on the floor.

"You get to see the house!" Preston's excitement was unmistakable, his grin stretching from ear to ear.

"Really? Is it finished?" Mary's eyes lit up as she clapped her hands in pure delight.

"Not quite," Preston admitted, "but it's ready enough for you to take a look!"

As soon as the construction began on the new house, Preston made her promise that she would stay away until it was done. Finally, two months later, the day arrived, and Mary couldn't wait.

"Lenore, are you going to come with us?" Mary asked as she draped her shawl over her shoulders.

"No, I think this is something you and Preston need to do yourselves. I'll watch Annie," Lenore said, smiled warmly.

Mary smiled and ran quickly into her bedroom, retrieving a large wooden box.

"What's that?" Preston asked, giving her a curious look.

"Never you mind. You'll see," Mary replied, smiling as she glanced over at Lenore.

Preston turned to her as they approached the road that led up to the house.

"Now close your eyes," he instructed.

Closing her eyes, Mary could feel her heartbeat inside her chest as the wagon turned the corner.

"Okay, open your eyes," Preston said, gently bringing the buggy to a stop.

Mary opened her eyes and gasped. The cabin stood proudly before her, exuding a sense of warmth and welcome. When they were preparing to rebuild, Preston had asked Mary what she wanted, and she had mentioned more windows and flower boxes. Now, two new windows were at the front, each adorned with a brand-new flower box.

"Preston, it's beautiful," Mary said, smiled and clapping her hands. "It's bigger than the old house and has an upstairs. It looks like the home I grew up in."

"Yes, I wanted you to feel completely at home," Preston said, jumping out of the wagon. "You wanted a new stone fireplace and more shelves, so we made it a bit bigger."

"Oh, Preston. I love it. When can we move in?"

"We'll be able to move in by the weekend," Preston said proudly. "Abe Turner will have the furniture finished by tomorrow, and the wood stove is being delivered the day after that."

"Can I see inside?" Mary asked eagerly, getting out of the wagon.

"Yes, there are a few more things left to do, but for the most part, it's done," Preston said proudly. "I think you'll like it."

Opening the door, Preston stood aside to let Mary walk in. The main room was L-shaped, with a staircase leading upstairs off to the side. The kitchen, which used to be centered around the fireplace, now stood separate in the far corner. Preston had built a large counter table for Mary to do her baking, and beside it was space for the new wood stove. Around the corner from the kitchen was a beautiful stone fireplace, giving the room a homey feel. Beside it, was a series of wooden shelves Mary had requested.

"Preston, I love the fireplace," she said, going over and touching the stone. "Where did you get all the stone?"

"Easy to find after a tornado, plus I made a few trips to the quarry," Preston said, smiling. "Are the shelves, okay?"

"They are perfect," Mary said, running her hand over the wood.

"I really hope you like everything," Preston said. "I wanted you to feel comfortable."

"Preston, it's beautiful," Mary beamed, giving him a hug. "This is going to be our home."

"Yes, it is," Preston laughed.

"I have my first surprise for you," Mary said. "Your turn to close your eyes."

"What? My first surprise? You mean you have two."

"Shush, now close your eyes," Mary said, quickly running out the door to the wagon.

Coming back in, she said, "Okay, open your eyes."

Preston opened his eyes and saw Mary holding the wooden box. "What's this?"

"Open the box," Mary said excitedly.

Preston opened the box and looked inside. Reaching in, he pulled out an old vase that had belonged to his mother. "Where did you get these? These are all my Ma's things."

"Remember that night I took them all down and you got so mad?" Mary asked.

"Yes, even if I care not to remember that night," Preston said, looking at her. "These were lost in the tornado."

"No, they weren't. Well, kind of. You see, that night you demanded I put them all back, I didn't. I was going to do it the next day, but then the storm hit. All these things were still in the box I had put in the barn for storage," Mary said. "I had Lenore bring me here the last time you went into town, and I found the box."

Preston looked at her and smiled. "I can't believe you came out here to look for this. I really thought these were lost."

"I thought a great spot for them in our new house would be on the shelves I asked for beside the fireplace," Mary said, smiling. "It could be a tribute to your mother's memory."

Preston looked at her with tears in his eyes. "I love that idea, and there is still plenty of room for our own memories."

"Yes, and room for a cradle, too, by the fireplace," Mary smiled.

"A cradle?" Preston said, looking at her. "Why would we need a cra... Mary, are you? Are you?"

"That's my second surprise. Yes, Preston. I am pregnant. I found out a few days ago," Mary said, grinning from ear to ear.

"I'm going to be a father?" Preston asked, looking at Mary in shock.

"Yes, and Annie is going to be a big sister," Mary said.

With tears running down his face, Preston went over and wrapped his arms around his wife. "I promise you that I will be the best husband and father. I have a lot to make up for, but I promise, Mary, you will never question my love for you and our life."

Mary, laying her head on Preston's chest and feeling the strength of his arms around her, knew her decision to move here was no longer a question. This is where she belonged, and this is where she planned to stay. She had a beautiful new home, a loving and wonderful husband, Annie, who she considered her daughter, and now a new baby growing inside her—not to mention new friends. Her life, which was once empty and lonely, was now filled with love, joy, warmth, and happiness.

She had finally found where she belonged, and it was right here, wrapped in Preston's arms, and she was never leaving.

Other books by Karen Leah Scott
THE DON'S TO SAYING I DO

LEAMINGVILLE MEADOWS SERIES
Comfort in the Sand Book 1
Comfort in the Sand Book 2
Tears and Secrets
Voices of Summer
Sierra's Light
A Snowball for Christmas
Just Friends
A Heart for Valentines Day

THORNBURY BROTHERS
Hunter
Drake

Conroy Manor
Promise Me
Tranquility Springs
Can I Borrow Your Dress

A Flamingo Named Frank
Don't forget to leave a review or a rating – it helps more than you realize.

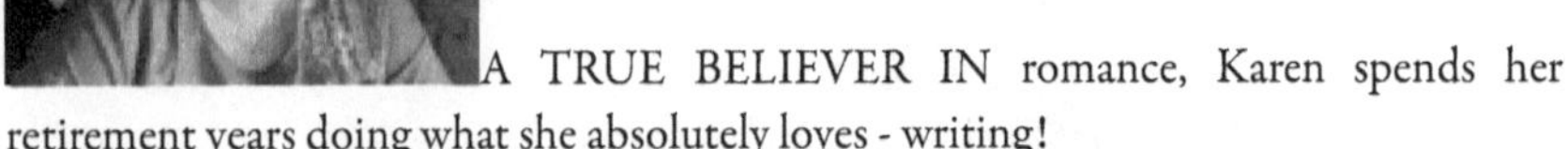

A TRUE BELIEVER IN romance, Karen spends her retirement years doing what she absolutely loves - writing!

After moving from Gatineau, Quebec, where she grew up, to the charming town of Leamington, Ontario, on the sunny shores of Lake Erie, Karen found endless inspiration in the sand and the waves. This lovely scenery sparked the creation of her delightful Leamingville Meadows Series.

When she's not crafting her next heartwarming story, Karen loves spending quality time with her husband, who is also her best friend. Life is a joy, and she's thrilled to share her literary world with you.

She doesn't ask for much, just for you to enjoy her books as much as she enjoys writing them. And if you feel so inclined, a review on Amazon would make her heart sing!

Happy Reading!